Great Stories From World Literature

Compiled by Doris Heitkotter
Illustrated by John Everds

Created by SYSTEMS FOR EDUCATION, Inc., *Chicago*
Published by THE SOUTHWESTERN COMPANY, *Nashville*

CONTENTS

Fables and
Mother Goose Rhymes

Fables are some of the oldest stories in the
world. They are very short, and usually
end with a wise saying or "lesson" that
pokes fun at the silly way people often
act. Thousands of years ago, a Greek slave
named Aesop wrote the fable you will read
here. It was the kind of story that poor
people told each other, laughing secretly
at men who were richer or bigger or
stronger than they were.

Mother Goose rhymes are also very old.
They were first put into a book about 250
years ago in England. No one is sure if
there really was an old lady named
"Mother Goose," but her rhymes are still
among everybody's favorites.

RAIN, RAIN, GO AWAY

Rain, rain, go away,
Come again another day.
Little Johnny wants to play.

Mother Goose Rhymes

IF

If all the world were apple pie,
  And all the sea were ink,
And all the trees were bread and cheese,
  What should we have for drink?

HEY! DIDDLE DIDDLE

Hey! Diddle diddle,
The cat and the fiddle,
The cow jumped over the moon.
The little dog laugh'd
To see such sport
And the dish ran away with the spoon.

HICKORY DICKORY DOCK

Hickory dickory dock,
The mouse ran up the clock.
The clock struck one,
The mouse ran down.
Hickory dickory dock.

THERE WAS A LITTLE GIRL

There was a little girl who had a little curl
Right in the middle of her forehead.
When she was good, she was very, very good,
And when she was bad she was horrid.

Old Mother Hubbard

Old Mother Hubbard
    Went to the cupboard,
To get her poor dog a bone:
    But when she got there
    The cupboard was bare,
And so the poor dog had none.

She went to the baker's
    To buy him some bread,
But when she came back
    The poor dog was dead.

8

She went to the joiner's
    To buy him a coffin,
But when she came back
    The poor dog was laughing.

She took a clean dish
    To get him some tripe,
But when she came back
    He was smoking a pipe.

The dame made a curtsey,
    The dog made a bow,
The dame said, "Your servant,"
    The dog said, "Bow-wow."

This wonderful dog
    Was Dame Hubbard's delight;
He could sing, he could dance,
    He could read, he could write.

She gave him rich dainties
    Whenever he fed,
And built him a monument
    When he was dead.

SARAH CATHERINE MARTIN

9

The Man, the Boy, and the Donkey

AESOP

A MAN AND HIS SON were going with their donkey to market. As they were walking along, a countryman passed them and said, "You fools, what is a donkey for but to ride upon?"

So the man put the boy on the donkey and they went on their way. Soon they passed a group of men. One of them said, "See that lazy youngster? He lets his father walk while he rides."

So the man ordered his boy to get off, and got on himself. They hadn't gone far when they passed two women. One woman said to the other, "Shame on that

lazy lout, to let his poor little son trudge along beside that big, strong donkey!"

Well, the man didn't know what to do. At last he took his boy up before him on the donkey. By this time they had come to the town. The passersby began to jeer and point at them. The man stopped and asked what they were scoffing at. The men said, "Aren't you ashamed of yourself for overloading that poor donkey of yours— you and your hulking son?"

The man and the boy got off and tried to think what to do. They thought and they thought. At last they cut down a pole, tied the donkey's feet to it, and raised the pole and the donkey to their shoulders. They went along amid the laughter of all who met them till they came to Market Bridge. The donkey, getting one of his feet loose, kicked out and caused the boy to drop his end of the pole. In the struggle the donkey fell over the bridge. His forefeet being tied together, he was drowned.

"That will teach you," said an old man who had followed them:

PLEASE ALL, AND YOU WILL PLEASE NONE.

Myths and Legends

Long ago, before people had a language they could read or write, they told stories. Many years later, other people wrote down these stories.

The stories we call myths were told about the gods and goddesses of the religions of these ancient people. There are many kinds of myths and legends, because there were many different religions. Myths come from China, from Mexico, from Greece and Rome, and from nearly every other country where people lived long ago.

One of the myths you will read here is about some Norse gods and giants. They appear in the myths from Scandinavia. The other is about some Greek heroes, who were a kind of "supermen" just a little less powerful than the gods.

The Three Golden Apples

NATHANIEL HAWTHORNE

Hercules was a great hero, known both for his strength and kindness. In return for the King of Greece's promise not to harm his stepfather, Hercules became the King's slave for ninety-nine months. The king did not like Hercules and gave him twelve dangerous Labors to do. For one of these Labors, Hercules was told to bring back three golden apples from the garden of the Hesperides. It was a dangerous mission because any mortal who picked one of these apples would immediately die. Hercules traveled far to find the garden, and on his way some nymphs told him that he should ask for help from Atlas, the giant who holds up the sky.

THE GIANT WAS AS TALL as a mountain. So vast was he that the clouds rested about his middle, like a belt, and hung like a beard from his chin, and flitted before his huge eyes, so that he could not see Hercules. And, most wonderful of all, the giant held up his great hands and appeared to support the sky, which so far as Hercules could see, rested on his head!

Just then a breeze blew away the clouds from before the giant's face. Poor fellow! He had evidently stood there a long while. An ancient forest had been growing and decaying around his feet, and oak trees six or seven centuries old had sprung from the acorn and forced themselves between his toes. The giant now looked down from the far height of his great eyes, and seeing

Hercules, roared out in a voice that resembled thunder, "Who are you, down at my feet there?"

"I am Hercules," thundered back the hero. "And I am seeking for the garden of the Hesperides!"

"I am Atlas, the mightiest giant in the world! And I hold the sky upon my head."

"So I see," answered Hercules. "But can you show me the way to the garden of the Hesperides?"

"What do you want there?" asked the giant.

"I want three of the golden apples," shouted Hercules. "For my master the King."

"There is nobody but myself," quoth the giant, "that can go to the garden of the Hesperides and gather the apples. If it were not for this little business of holding up the sky, I would make half a dozen steps across the sea, and get them for you."

"Is the sky very heavy?" Hercules inquired.

"Why, not particularly so, at first," answered the giant, shrugging his shoulders. "But it gets to be after a thousand years!"

"And how long a time," asked the hero, "will it take you to get the golden apples?"

"Oh, that will be done in a few moments!" cried Atlas. "I will take ten or fifteen miles at a stride, and be at the garden and back again before your shoulders begin to ache."

"Well, then," answered Hercules, "I will climb the mountain behind you there, and relieve you of your burden." Without more words, the sky was shifted from the shoulders of Atlas and placed upon those of Hercules. Then Atlas stepped into the sea. His first stride covered ten miles. Hercules watched the giant as he went onward. It was a wonderful sight. But, as the gigantic shape faded entirely out of view, Hercules realized that the weight of the sky was already a little irksome to his shoulders.

"I really pity the poor giant," thought Hercules. "If it tires me so much in ten minutes, how it must have tired him in a thousand years."

I know not how long it was before, to his unspeakable joy, he beheld the huge shape of the giant. At his approach, Atlas held up his hand, in which Hercules could see three magnificent golden apples, as big as pumpkins, all hanging from one branch.

"I am glad to see you again," shouted Hercules. "So you have got the golden apples?"

"Certainly," answered Atlas, "and very fair apples they are. I took the finest that grew on the tree, I assure you."

"You have had a pleasant ramble and I heartily thank you for your trouble," said Hercules, "and now, as I have a long way to go, and am rather in haste, will you be kind enough to take the sky off my shoulders again?"

"Why, as to that," said the giant, "I have no fancy for burdening myself with the sky just now."

"What!" shouted Hercules. "Do you intend to make me bear this burden forever?"

"We will see about that one of these days," answered the giant. "At all events, you ought not to complain if you have to bear it the next hundred years, or perhaps the next thousand. I bore it a good while longer, in spite of the backache. Well, then, after a thousand years, if I happen to feel in the mood, we may possibly shift about again. You are certainly a very strong man, and can never have a better opportunity to prove it."

Hercules, being as clever as he was strong, said to the giant, "Just take the sky upon your head one instant, will you? I want to make a cushion of my lion's skin for the weight to rest on. It really chafes me, and will cause unnecessary inconvenience in so many centuries as I am to stand here."

"That's no more than fair, and I'll do it!" said the giant. "For just five minutes, then, I'll take back the sky. Only for five minutes, remember! I have no idea of spending another thousand years as I spent the last. Variety is the spice of life, I say!"

Ah, the thick-witted old rogue of a giant! He threw down the golden apples and received back the sky from the head and shoulders of Hercules onto his own, where it rightly belonged. And Hercules picked up the three golden apples and set out on his journey homeward.

And there stands the giant to this day, or, at any rate, there stands a mountain as tall as he, which bears his name. And when the thunder rumbles we may imagine it to be the voice of the Giant Atlas, bellowing after Hercules who tricked him.

The Quest of the Hammer

ABBIE FARWELL BROWN

In Norse mythology, the gods, called the Aesir, lived in their heaven which they called Asgard. The chief god was Odin, and he had brothers and sisters and many children, one of whom was Thor, the Thunder Lord. Thor controlled the weather on earth, and protected the palaces of Asgard with his magic hammer, which was called Miölnir. This story tells about the time Thor lost his hammer.

ONE MORNING THOR the Thunderer awoke with a yawn and, stretching out his knotted arm, felt for his precious hammer, which he kept always under his pillow of clouds. He started up with a roar of rage. The hammer was gone!

Now this was a very serious matter, for Thor was the protector of Asgard. Miölnir, the magic hammer, was his mighty weapon, of which the enemies of the Aesir stood so much in dread that they dared not venture near. But if they should learn that Miölnir was gone, who could tell what danger might not threaten the palaces of heaven?

"It is Loki again!" he cried. "I am sure Loki is at the bottom of this mischief!" But this time Thor was mistaken. It was not Loki who had stolen the hammer—he was too great a coward for that.

Loki protested that he had nothing to do with so wicked a deed. "But," he added, "I think I can guess the thief and I will help you to find him."

Loki drew near and whispered in Thor's ear. "It is Thrym, the mighty giant who has ever been your enemy and your imitator, and whose fingers have long itched to grasp the mighty Miölnir, that the world might name him Thunder Lord instead of you."

Then Thor roared with rage. "I will seek this impudent Thrym and crush him into bits!"

"Softly, softly," said Loki, smiling maliciously. "He is a shrewd giant. You must use craft, and it is I who will teach you, if you will be patient."

Thor was a brave, blunt fellow, and he hated the ways of Loki, his lies and his deceit. But without the hammer he could not fight the giants hand to hand.

Loki was all eagerness, for he loved difficulties which would set his wit in play and bring other folk into danger.

"Look, now," he said, "we must go to Freia and borrow her falcon dress."

So first they made their way to the house of maidens, where Freia dwelt, and borrowed the magic dress of feathers in which Freia would clothe herself and flit like a great beautiful bird all about the world.

"Now I will fetch the hammer for you," said Loki. So he put on the falcon plumage and flapped away to the dark country. This was Jotunheim, the land of the Frost Giants.

When Loki came there he found Thrym the Giant King sitting outside his palace cave. "Loki!" said Thrym, "how dare you venture alone in this guise to Giant Land?"

"It is an ill day in Asgard," sighed Loki, keeping his eye warily upon the giant. "Some mighty one has stolen the hammer of our Thor. Is it you, Thrym? Greatest of all giants, greater than Thor himself?"

This the crafty one said to flatter Thrym, for Loki well knew the weakness of those who love to be thought greater than they are.

"Miölnir the hammer is mine," said Thrym, "and I am Thunder Lord, mightiest of the mighty. I have hidden it where Thor can never find it. But listen, Loki. Go tell the Aesir that I will give it back upon one condition—that they send Freia the beautiful to be my wife."

"Freia the beautiful!" Loki had to stifle a laugh. Fancy the Aesir giving their fairest flower to such an ugly fellow as this! But he only said politely, "It is a costly price, great Thrym, but if I have my way, you shall soon see the fairest bride in all the world knocking at your door."

So Loki whizzed back to Asgard on his falcon wings. Now you can imagine the horror that was in Asgard as everyone listened to Loki's words, for Freia was fairer than fair and sweeter than sweet.

Then spoke Heimdal who was the wisest of the Aesir, for he could see into the future and knew how things would come to pass. "I have a plan," he said. "Let us dress Thor himself like a bride in Freia's robes and send him to Jotunheim to talk with Thrym and to win back his hammer."

But at these words Thor grew angry. "What! dress me like a girl!" he roared. "I will fight! I will die, if need be! But dressed as a woman I will not go!"

But Loki answered him with sharp words, for this was a scheme after his own heart. "What, Thor!" he said. "Would you lose your hammer and keep Asgard in danger for so small a whim? Heimdal's plan is a good one, and I myself will help to carry it out."

Still Thor hesitated, but Freia came and laid her white hand on his arm, and looked up into his scowling

face pleadingly. "To save me, Thor," she begged. And Thor said he would go.

Then there was great sport among the Aesir, while they dressed Thor like a beautiful maiden. They let out seams, and let down hems. They hid Thor's great limbs and knotted arms under Freia's fairest robe of scarlet. Freia herself twisted about his neck her famous necklace of starry jewels, and hung at his belt a jingling bunch of keys, as was the custom for the bride to wear at Norse weddings. Last of all, they threw over him a long veil of silver white which covered him to the feet. And there he stood, as stately and tall a bride as even a giant might wish to see. But on his hands he wore his iron gloves, and they ached for but one thing—to grasp the handle of the stolen hammer.

"Come," said Thor sulkily to Loki, "it is fitting that you go dressed as my handmaiden, for I like not these lies and maskings, and I may spoil the masquerade without you at my elbow."

Thrym heard the sound of their approach, for his ear was eager. "Hola!" he cried. "Hasten, men, and see if they are bringing Freia to be my wife." Then the lookout giant stepped down from the top of his mountain, and said that a chariot was bringing two maidens to the palace door.

"Run, giants, run!" shouted Thrym, in a fever at this news. "My bride is coming."

That evening there was a wonderful banquet to celebrate the wedding. Now Thor's long journey had made him very hungry. First under the silver veil disappeared by pieces a whole roast ox. Then Thor was thirsty, and one after another he raised to his lips and emptied three great barrels of mead. Thrym was amazed, for Thor's giant appetite had beaten that of the giants themselves.

"Never before saw I a bride so hungry," he cried, "and never before one half so thirsty!"

But Loki, the waiting maid, whispered to him softly, "The truth is, great Thrym, that my dear mistress was almost starved. For eight days Freia has eaten nothing at all, so eager was she for Jotunheim."

Thrym was delighted. He forgave his hungry bride, and loved her with all his heart. He longed to call her his very own dear wife. "Bring in the wedding gift!" he cried. "Bring in Thor's hammer, Miölnir, and give it

to Freia, as I promised. For when I have kept my word, she will be mine—all mine!"

Then Thor's big heart laughed under his woman's dress. His fierce eyes swept eagerly down the hall to meet the servant who was bringing in the hammer on a velvet cushion. The giant servant drew nearer, puffing and blowing, strong though he was, beneath the mighty weight. Thor's heart swelled, and he gave a most unmaidenly shout of rage and triumph. With one swoop he grasped the hammer in his iron fingers. With the other arm he tore off the veil that hid his terrible face, and trampled it under foot. Then he turned to the frightened king, who cowered beside him on the throne.

"Thief!" he cried. "Freia sends you *this* as a wedding gift!" And he whirled the hammer about his head, then hurled it once, twice, thrice, as it rebounded to his hand. In the first stroke, as of lightning, Thrym rolled dead from his throne. In the second stroke perished the whole giant household. In the third stroke, the palace itself tumbled together and fell to the ground.

But Loki and Thor stood safely among the ruins, dressed in their tattered maiden robes, a quaint and curious sight. And Loki, full of mischief now as ever, burst out laughing.

Thor held up his hammer and shook it gently as he said, "I have my hammer again and the joke is done."

Loki heard and stifled his laughter as best he could. For it is not good to laugh at him who holds the hammer. Not once after that was there mention in Asgard of the time when Thor dressed as a girl and won his bridal gift from Thrym the giant.

Fairy Tales

Fairy tales are stories about wonderful, faraway worlds where magic things happen every day. Animals talk and act like people. Witches cast magic spells. Kings and princes and princesses live in tall castles in deep forests.

Most fairy tales are old, old stories that some good storytellers have written down for everyone to read and enjoy. Here are two stories by several of the most famous storytellers in the world — Hans Christian Andersen, who was Danish, and Jacob and Wilhelm Grimm, who were two brothers from Germany.

Just use your imagination and enjoy the make-believe worlds they wrote about!

The Frog Prince

JACOB AND WILHELM GRIMM

IN THE OLDEN TIME, when wishing was having, there lived a King whose daughters were all beautiful. But the youngest was so exceedingly beautiful that the Sun himself was enchanted every time she came out into the sunshine.

Near the castle of this King was a large and gloomy forest, and in the midst stood an old lime tree, beneath whose branches splashed a little fountain. So whenever it was very hot, the King's youngest daughter ran off into this wood, and sat down by the side of this fountain. When she was bored, she would often divert herself by

throwing a golden ball up in the air and catching it. And this was her favorite amusement.

Now one day it happened that when the Princess threw this golden ball into the air, it did not fall down into her hand, but on the grass. Then it rolled past her into the fountain. The King's daughter followed the ball with her eyes, but it disappeared beneath the water, which was so deep that no one could see to the bottom. She began to cry louder and louder. As she cried, a voice called out, "Why weepest thou, O King's daughter? Thy tears would melt even a stone to pity." And she looked around to the spot whence the voice came, and saw a frog stretching his thick ugly head out of the water.

"You old water-paddler," said she, "was it you that spoke? I am weeping for my golden ball which has slipped away from me into the water."

"Be quiet and do not cry," answered the Frog. "I can give thee good advice. But what wilt thou give me if I fetch thy plaything up again?"

"What will you have, dear Frog?" said she. "My dresses, my pearls and jewels, or the golden crown which I wear?"

The Frog answered, "Dresses, or jewels, or golden crowns are not for me. But if thou wilt love me, and let me be thy companion and playfellow, and sit at thy table, and eat from thy little golden plate, and drink out of thy cup, and sleep in thy little bed—if thou wilt promise me all these, then will I dive down and fetch up thy golden ball."

"Oh, I will promise you all," said she, "if only you will get me my ball." But she thought to herself, "What is the silly Frog chattering about? Let him remain in the water with his equals. He cannot mix in society." But the Frog, as soon as he had received her promise, drew his head under the water and dived down. Presently he swam up again with the ball in his mouth, and threw it on the grass. The King's daughter was full of joy when she again saw her beautiful plaything. Taking it up, she ran off immediately.

"Stop! stop!" cried the Frog. "Take me with thee. I can't run as thou canst." But his croaking was useless. Although it was loud enough, the King's daughter did not hear it. Hastening home, she soon forgot the poor Frog, who was obliged to leap back into the fountain.

The next day, when the King's daughter was sitting at table with her father and all his courtiers, and was eating from her own little golden plate, something was

heard coming up the marble stairs, *splish-splash, splish-splash.* When it arrived at the top, it knocked at the door, and a voice said, "Open the door, thou youngest daughter of the King!"

She rose and went to see who it was that called her. But when she opened the door and caught sight of the Frog, she shut it again, and sat down at the table, looking very pale. But the King saw that her heart was beating violently, and asked her whether it were a giant who had come to fetch her away who stood at the door. "Oh, no!" she answered. "It is no giant, but an ugly Frog."

"What does the Frog want with you?" said the King.

"Oh, dear father, when I was sitting yesterday playing by the fountain, my golden ball fell into the water. This Frog fetched it up again because I cried so much, but first I must tell you, he pressed me so much, that I promised him he should be my companion. I never thought he could come out of the water, but somehow he has jumped out, and now he wants to come in here."

At that moment there was another knock, and a voice said:

"King's daughter, youngest,
Open the door.
Hast thou forgotten
Thy promises made
At the fountain so clear?
'Neath the lime-tree's shade?
King's daughter, youngest,
Open the door."

Then the King said, "What you have promised, that you must perform. Go and let him in." So the King's daughter went and opened the door. The Frog hopped in after her right up to her chair.

As soon as she was seated the Frog said, "Take me up." But she hesitated so long that at last the King ordered her to obey. And as soon as the Frog sat on the chair he jumped on to the table and said, "Now push thy plate near me, that we may eat together." And she

did so, but as everyone saw, very unwillingly. The Frog seemed to relish his dinner much, but every bite that the King's daughter ate nearly choked her, till at last the Frog said, "I have satisfied my hunger and feel very tired. Wilt thou carry me upstairs now into thy chamber, and make thy bed ready that we may sleep together?" At this speech the King's daughter began to cry, for she was afraid of the cold Frog, and dared not touch him. Besides, he actually wanted to sleep in her own beautiful, clean bed.

But her tears only made the King angry. He said, "He helped you in the time of your trouble, and must not now be despised!"

So she took the Frog up with two fingers, and put him in a corner of her chamber. But as she lay in her bed, he crept up to it, and said, "I am so very tired that I shall sleep well. Do take me up or I will tell thy father."

This speech made the King's daughter terribly angry. Catching the Frog up, she threw him with all her strength against the wall, saying, "Now will you be quiet, you ugly Frog!"

But as he fell he was changed from a frog into a handsome Prince with beautiful eyes. After a little while, he became, with her father's consent, her dear companion and betrothed. Then he told her how he had been transformed by an evil witch, and that no one but herself could have had the power to take him out of the fountain. And soon they were married and went together into the Prince's own kingdom.

The Nightingale

HANS CHRISTIAN ANDERSEN

THE EMPEROR'S PALACE was the most magnificent palace in the world. It was made entirely of fine porcelain. The choicest flowers were to be seen in the garden. Everything in the Emperor's garden was excellently well-arranged. Whoever walked beyond it, however, came to a beautiful wood with very high trees, and beyond that, to a lake. Large vessels could sail close under the branches. Among the branches dwelt a Nightingale, who sang so sweetly that even the poor fisherman, who had so much else to do, would stand still and listen. "Oh, how pretty that is!" he would say, and then go back to his work.

Travellers came from all parts of the world to see the Emperor's city, the palace, and the garden. But if they heard the Nightingale, they said, "This is the best of all." Learned men wrote books about the city, the palace, and the garden. Nor did they forget the Nightingale. She was praised above everything else.

These books reached the Emperor. He read and read, and nodded his head. These splendid descriptions of the city, the palace, and the garden pleased him greatly. "But there is nothing like the Nightingale," said the book.

"What in the world is this?" said the Emperor. "The Nightingale! I do not know it at all! Can there be such a bird in my empire, in my garden even, without my having heard of it? Truly, one may learn something from books."

So he called his Gentleman Usher, who was so grand a personage that no one of inferior rank might speak to him. "There is said to be a very remarkable bird here, called the Nightingale," said the Emperor. "Her song, they say, is worth more than anything else in all my dominions. Why has no one ever told me of her?"

"I have never before heard her mentioned," said the Gentleman Usher. "She has never been presented at court."

"I wish her to come and sing before me this evening," said the Emperor. "The whole world knows what I have, and I do not know it myself. I wish to hear the Nightingale. She must be here this evening. If she doesn't come, after supper the whole court will be flogged."

"Tsing-pe!" exclaimed the Gentleman Usher. He ran upstairs and downstairs, and half the court ran with him. No one would have relished the flogging. Many were the questions asked about the wonderful Nightingale, whom the whole world talked of, and about whom no one at the court knew anything.

At last they met a poor little girl in the kitchen, who said, "Oh, yes, the Nightingale! I know her very well.

Oh, how she can sing! Every evening, when I rest in the wood, I hear her. It makes the tears come into my eyes."

"Little Kitchen-maiden," said the Gentleman Usher, "will you conduct us to the Nightingale? She is expected at court this evening."

So they went together to the wood, where the Nightingale was accustomed to sing.

"There she is!" said the little girl. "Listen! listen! There she sits." She pointed to a little gray bird up in the branches.

"Most excellent Nightingale," said the Gentleman Usher, "I have the honor to invite you to a court festival, which is to take place this evening. His Imperial Majesty will doubtless be enchanted with your delightful song."

"With the greatest pleasure," replied the Nightingale, "but my song would sound far better among the green trees." However, she followed willingly because she knew that the Emperor wished it.

In the midst of the grand hall, where the Emperor sat, a golden perch was erected on which the Nightingale was to sit.

And the Nightingale sang so sweetly that tears came into the Emperor's eyes. She sang more sweetly still, and tears rolled down his cheeks.

The Nightingale's success was complete. She was now to remain in court.

One day a large parcel arrived for the Emperor, on which was written, "Nightingale."

"Here we have another new book about our far-famed bird," said the Emperor. But it was not a book. It was a little piece of mechanism, lying in a box. It was

an artificial nightingale, which was intended to look like the living one. But it was covered all over with diamonds, rubies, and sapphires. When this artificial bird had been wound up, it could sing one of the tunes that the real Nightingale sang.

"Now they shall sing together. We will have a duet," said everyone. And so they must sing together. But it did not succeed, for the real Nightingale sang in her own way, and the artificial bird produced its tones by wheels. "It is not his fault," said the artist. "He keeps exact time and quite according to the method."

So the artificial bird must sing alone. He was quite as successful as the real Nightingale. And then he was so much prettier to look at. His plumage sparkled with jewels. His silver and gold tail moved up and down.

Thirty-three times he sang one and the same tune, and yet he was not weary. Everyone would willingly have heard him again. However, the Emperor now wished the real Nightingale to sing something—but where was she? No one had remarked that she had flown out of the open window—flown away to her own green wood.

"What is the meaning of this?" said the Emperor. All of the courtiers abused the Nightingale and called her a most ungrateful creature. "We have the best bird, at all events," they said. And for the thirty-fourth time they heard the same tune. The artist praised the bird inordinately and received permission to show the bird to the people on the following Sunday. But the fisher-man, who had heard the real Nightingale, said, "It sounds

very pretty, almost like the real bird. But yet there is something wanting—I know not what."

The real Nightingale was banished from the empire.

The artificial bird had his place on a silken cushion, close to the Emperor's bed. His place was number one on the left side. For the Emperor thought that the side where the heart was situated must be the place of honor, and the heart is situated on the left side of an Emperor, as well as with other folks.

Thus it went on for a whole year. But one evening there was suddenly a noise, "Bang!" inside the bird. Then something sprang, "Sur-r-r." All the wheels were running about, and the music stopped.

The Emperor quickly jumped out of bed, and had his chief physician called. But what good could he be? Then the clockmaker was called. At last, after a great deal of discussion and consultation, the bird was in some measure put to rights again. But the clockmaker said he must be spared much singing. Now the artificial bird was allowed to sing only once a year.

When five years were passed, a great sadness visited the whole empire. In their hearts the people thought highly of their Emperor, and now he was ill. It was reported he could not live. A new Emperor had already been chosen, and the people stood in the street outside the palace.

Cold and pale lay the Emperor in his magnificent bed. A window was opened above and the moon shone down on the Emperor and the artificial bird.

The poor Emperor could scarcely breathe. It appeared to him as though something were sitting on his chest. He opened his eyes, and saw that it was Death, who had put on the Emperor's crown.

"Music, music!" cried the Emperor. "Thou dear little artificial bird! Sing, I pray thee, sing! I have given thee gold and precious stones. Sing, I pray thee, sing."

But the bird was silent. There was no one there to wind him up. Death continued to stare at the Emperor with his great hollow eyes. Everywhere it was still, fearfully still!

All at once the sweetest song was heard from the window. It was the little living Nightingale who was

sitting on a branch outside. She had heard of the Emperor's severe illness, and came to sing to him of comfort and hope. As she sang, the blood flowed more quickly through the Emperor's feeble limbs, and even Death listened and said, "Go on, little Nightingale, go on."

"Wilt thou give me the splendid gold Crown of the Emperor?" And Death gave up this treasure for a song. And the Nightingale sang on as Death flew out at the window like a cold, white shadow.

"Thanks, thanks!" said the Emperor. "Thou heavenly little bird, I know thee well! I have banished thee from my realm, and thou hast sung away death from my heart. How shall I reward thee?"

"Thou hast already rewarded me," said the Nightingale. "I have seen tears in thine eyes, as when I sang to thee for the first time. Those I shall never forget. They are jewels which do so much good to a minstrel's heart. But sleep now, and wake fresh and healthy. I will sing thee to sleep."

And she sang—and the Emperor fell into a sweet sleep. Oh, how soft and kindly was that sleep!

The sun shone in at the window when he awoke, strong and healthy. Not one of his servants had returned, for they all believed him dead. But the Nightingale still sat and sang.

The attendants came to look at their dead Emperor, and the Emperor said, "Good morning!"

Adventure

Who wouldn't like to sail on a pirate ship?
Explore a jungle? Climb a mountain?
Fly an airplane? Take a rocket to the
moon?

The next three stories are about *adventure*.
They happen at different times and in
different parts of the world. Mowgli's
adventures are in the jungles of India.
Robin Hood and Jim Hawkins are both
English. All three of them have many more
adventures that are told in the complete
books these stories come from.

The adventures you have will probably be
very different from these. But sometimes
it is almost as exciting to read about
adventures as it is to have them!

Mowgli's Brothers

RUDYARD KIPLING

FATHER WOLF LISTENED. Below in the valley that ran down to a little river, he heard the dry, angry, snarly, singsong whine of a tiger. "The fool!" said Father Wolf. "To begin a night's work with that noise!"

"H'sh! It is neither bullock nor buck he hunts to-night," said Mother Wolf. "It is Man."

"Man!" said Father Wolf, showing all his teeth. "Faugh! Are there not enough beetles and frogs in the tanks that he must eat Man, and on our ground too!"

The purr grew louder, and ended in the full-throated "Aaarh!" of the tiger's charge.

Then there was a howl—an untigerish howl—from Shere Khan. "He has missed," said Mother Wolf. "What is it?"

Father Wolf ran out a few paces. "The fool had no more sense than to jump at a woodcutter's camp fire, and has burned his feet," said Father Wolf, with a grunt.

"Something is coming up hill," said Mother Wolf, twitching one ear. "Get ready."

The bushes rustled a little in the thicket, and Father Wolf dropped with his haunches under him, ready for his leap. He jumped—and then stopped in mid-spring.

"Man!" he snapped. "A man's cub. Look!"

Directly in front of him, holding on by a low branch, stood a naked brown baby who could just walk. He looked

47

up into Father Wolf's face and laughed. "Is that a man's cub?" said Mother Wolf. "I have never seen one. Bring it here."

Father Wolf's jaws closed right on the child's back, and not a tooth even scratched the skin as he laid it down among the cubs.

"How little! How naked and—how bold!" said Mother Wolf, softly. The baby was pushing his way between the cubs to get close to the warm hide. "So this is a man's cub. Now, was there ever a wolf that could boast of a man's cub among her children?"

"I have heard now and again of such a thing, but never in our Pack or in my time," said Father Wolf. "He is altogether without hair, and I could kill him with a touch of my foot. But see, he looks up and is not afraid."

The moonlight was blocked out of the mouth of the cave, for Shere Khan's great square head and shoulders were thrust into the entrance. Father Wolf was very angry. "What does Shere Khan need?" he growled.

"My quarry. A man's cub went this way," said Shere Khan. "Its parents have run off. Give it to me."

Father Wolf knew that the mouth of the cave was too narrow for a tiger to come in by. "The wolves are a free people," said Father Wolf. "They take orders from the Head of the Pack, and not from any striped cattle-killer. The man's cub is ours—to kill if we choose."

"Ye choose and ye do not choose! What talk is this of choosing? By the bull that I killed, am I to stand nosing into your dog's den for my fair dues? It is I, Shere Khan, who speak!"

The tiger's roar filled the cave with thunder. Mother Wolf shook herself clear of the cubs and sprang forward, her eyes, like two green moons in the darkness, facing the blazing eyes of Shere Khan.

"And it is I, Raksha the Demon, who answer. The man's cub is mine. He shall not be killed. He shall live to run with the Pack and to hunt with the Pack. And in the end, look you, hunter of little naked cubs—he shall hunt thee! Now get thee hence! Go!"

Shere Khan might have faced Father Wolf, but he could not stand up against Mother Wolf, for he knew that where she was she had all the advantage of the

ground, and would fight to the death. So he backed out of the cave-mouth growling, and when he was clear he shouted:

"Each dog barks in his own yard! We will see what the Pack will say to this fostering of man-cubs. The cub is mine, and to my teeth will come in the end, O bush-tailed thieves!"

Mother Wolf threw herself down panting among the cubs, and Father Wolf said to her gravely:

"Shere Khan speaks this much truth. The cub must be shown to the Pack."

The Law of the Jungle lays down very clearly that any wolf may, when he marries, withdraw from the Pack he belongs to. But as soon as his cubs are old enough to stand on their feet he must bring them to the Pack Council, which is generally held once a month at full moon, in order that the other wolves may identify them. After that, the cubs are free to run as they please.

Father Wolf waited till his cubs could run a little, and then on the night of the Pack Meeting took them, and Mowgli the man-cub, and Mother Wolf to the Council Rock. Akela, the great, gray Lone Wolf, who led all the Pack by strength and cunning, lay out at full length on his rock, and below him sat forty or more wolves of every size and color. There was very little talking at the rock. The cubs tumbled over each other in the center of the circle where their mothers and fathers sat. Sometimes a mother wolf would push her cub far out into the moonlight, to be sure that he had not been overlooked. Akela from his rock would cry, "Ye know the Law—ye know the Law. Look well, O Wolves!"

50

And the anxious mothers would take up the call, "Look—look well, O Wolves!"

At last Father Wolf pushed Mowgli, called "the Frog," into the center, where he sat laughing and playing with some pebbles that glistened in the moonlight.

Akela never raised his head from his paws, but went on with the monotonous cry, "Look well!" A muffled roar came up from behind the rocks—the voice of Shere Khan crying, "The cub is mine. Give him to me. What have the Free People to do with a man's cub?"

Akela never even twitched his ears. All he said was, "Look well, O Wolves! What have the Free People to do with the orders of any save the Free People? Look well!"

There was a chorus of deep growls, and a young wolf in his fourth year flung back Shere Khan's question. "What have the Free People to do with a man's cub?"

Now the Law of the Jungle lays down that if there is any dispute as to the right of a cub to be accepted by the Pack, he must be spoken for by at least two members of the Pack who are not his father and mother.

"Who speaks for this cub?" said Akela. "Among the Free People who speaks?" There was no answer, and Mother Wolf got ready for what she knew would be her last fight, if things came to fighting.

Then the only other creature who is allowed at the Pack Council—Baloo, the sleepy brown bear who teaches the wolf cubs the Law of the Jungle—rose up on his hindquarters and grunted. "I speak for the man's cub. There is no harm in a man's cub. Let him run with the Pack, and be entered with the others. I myself will teach him."

"We need yet another," said Akela. "Baloo has spoken. Who speaks besides Baloo?"

A black shadow dropped down into the circle. It was Bagheera the inky black panther. Everybody knew Bagheera, and nobody cared to cross his path, for he was as cunning as a jackal, as bold as a wild buffalo, and as reckless as a wounded elephant. But he had a voice as soft as wild honey dripping from a tree.

"O Akela, and ye the Free People," he purred, "I have no right in your assembly, but the Law of the Jungle says that if there is doubt which is not a killing matter in regard to a new cub, the life of that cub may be bought at a price. And the law does not say who may or may not pay that price. Am I right?"

"Good! Good!" said the young wolves, who are always hungry. "Listen to Bagheera. The cub can be bought for a price. It is the Law."

Bagheera continued, "To kill a naked cub is shame. Besides, he may make better sport for you when he is grown. Baloo has spoken in his behalf. Now to Baloo's word I will add one bull, and a fat one, newly killed, not half a mile from here, if ye will accept the man's cub."

There was a clamor of scores of voices saying, "What matter? He will die in the winter rains. He will scorch in the sun. What harm can a naked frog do us? Let him run with the Pack. Where is the bull, Bagheera? Let him be accepted."

Shere Khan roared in the night, for he was very angry that Mowgli had not been handed over to him.

"Ay, roar well," said Bagheera, under his whiskers, "for the time comes when this naked thing will make thee roar to another tune, or I know nothing of man."

"It was well done," said Akela. "Men and their cubs are very wise. He may be a help in time. Take him away," he said to Father Wolf, "and train him as befits one of the Free People."

And that is how Mowgli was entered into the See-onee wolf pack, at the price of a bull and on Baloo's good word.

The Shooting Match
at Nottingham

HOWARD PYLE

WHEN ROBIN HOOD first heard the news, he was in Lincoln Town. Hastening back to Sherwood Forest, he soon called all his merry men about him and spoke to them thus:

"Now hearken, my merry men all, to the news that I have brought from Lincoln Town today. Our friend the Sheriff of Nottingham hath proclaimed a shooting match and hath sent messengers to tell of it through all the countryside. The prize is to be a bright golden arrow. Now I would have one of us win it, both because of the fairness of the prize and because our friend the Sheriff hath offered it. So we will take our bows and shafts and go there to shoot, for I know right well that merriment will be a-going. What say ye, lads?"

Then young David of Doncaster spoke up and said, "Listen, I pray thee, good master, unto what I say. This knavish Sheriff hath laid a trap for thee in this shooting match and wishes nothing so much as to see thee there. So go not, good master, for I know well he doth seek to beguile thee. Stay within the greenwood lest we all meet dole and woe."

"Now," quoth Robin, "thou art a wise lad, and keepest thine ears open and thy mouth shut, as becometh a wise and crafty woodsman. But shall we let it be said that the Sheriff of Nottingham did cow bold Robin Hood

and his sevenscore as fair archers as are in all merry England? Nay, good David, what thou tellest me maketh me to desire the prize even more than I else should do. Therefore we must meet guile with guile. Now some of you clothe yourselves as rustic peasants, and some as tinkers, or as beggars. But see that each man taketh a good bow, in case need should arise. As for myself, I will shoot for this same golden arrow. How like you the plan, my merry men all?"

"Good, good!" cried all the band heartily.

A fair sight was Nottingham Town on the day of the shooting match. And never was such a company of yeoman as were gathered that day, for the very best archers of merry England had come to this match.

When the Sheriff and his dame had sat down, he bade his herald sound three blasts that came echoing cheerily back from the gray walls of Nottingham. The archers stepped forth to their places. Then the herald stood forth and loudly proclaimed the rules of the game as follows:

"One arrow shooteth each man first, and from all the archers shall the ten that shooteth the fairest shafts be choosen for to shoot again. Of these ten, shall the

three that shoot the fairest shafts be chosen for to shoot again. Three arrows shooteth each man of those three, and to him that shooteth the fairest shafts shall the prize be given."

Now the archers shot, each man in turn, and the good folk never saw such archery as was done that day. When the last arrow sped and struck the target, all the people shouted aloud, for it was noble shooting.

And now but ten men were left of all those that had shot before. Of these ten, six were famous throughout the land.

Then the Sheriff leaned forward, looking keenly among the archers to find whether Robin Hood was among them, but no one was there clad in Lincoln green, such as Robin and his band wore. "Now," quoth he to a man-at-arms who stood near him, "seest thou Robin Hood among those ten?"

"Nay, that do I not, your Worship," answered the man. "Six of them I know right well. Of the others, one is too tall and the other too short for that bold knave. Robin's beard is as yellow as gold, while yon tattered beggar in scarlet hath a beard of brown, besides being blind of one eye."

"Then," quoth the Sheriff, smiting his thigh angrily, "yon knave is a coward as well as a rogue, and dares not show his face among good men and true."

And now but three men were left of all those that had shot before. "Now shoot thou well, Gilbert," cried the Sheriff, "and if thine be the best shaft, fivescore broad silver pennies will I give to thee beside the prize."

"Truly, I will do my best," quoth Gilbert. So saying, he drew forth a fair smooth arrow and, drawing his bow with care, he sped the shaft. Straight flew the arrow and lit fairly in the clout, a finger's breadth from the center.

"Now, by my faith," cried the Sheriff, "that is a shrewd shot!"

Then the tattered stranger stepped forth, and all the people laughed as they saw a yellow patch that showed beneath his arm when he raised his elbow to shoot, and also to see him aim with but one eye. He drew the good

yew bow quickly, and quickly loosed a shaft. So short was the time that no man could draw a breath betwixt the drawing and the shooting. Yet his arrow lodged nearer the center than the other by twice the length of a barleycorn.

Then Adam o' the Dell shot, carefully and cautiously, and his arrow lodged close beside the stranger's. After a short space they all three shot again, and once more

the tattered stranger's shot was the best. Then after another time of rest, they all shot for the third time. This time Gilbert took great heed to his aim, keenly measuring the distance and shooting with shrewdest care. Straight flew the arrow, and the shaft lodged close beside the spot that marked the very center.

"Well done, Gilbert!" cried the Sheriff right joyously. "Now, thou ragged knave, let me see thee shoot a better shaft than that!"

Nought spoke the stranger but took his place. He drew his trusty yew, holding it drawn but a moment, then loosed the string. Straight flew the arrow, and so true that it smote a gray goose feather from off Gilbert's shaft, which fell fluttering through the sunlit air as the stranger's arrow lodged in the very center. No one spoke a word for a while and no one shouted, but each man looked into his neighbor's face amazedly.

"Nay," quoth old Adam o' the Dell presently, drawing a long breath and shaking his head as he spoke, "I shoot no more today, for no man can match with yon stranger, whosoe'er he may be."

Then the Sheriff came down and drew near, in all his silks and velvets, to where the tattered stranger stood leaning upon his stout bow. "Here, good fellow," quoth the Sheriff, "take thou the prize, and well and fairly hast thou won it, I trow. What may be thy name, and whence comest thou?"

"Men do call me Jock o' Teviotdale, and thence am I come," said the stranger.

"Then, by Our Lady, Jock, thou art the fairest archer that e'er mine eyes beheld, and if thou wilt join my service, I will clothe thee with a better coat than thou hast

upon thy back. Thou shalt eat and drink of the best. I trow thou drawest better bow than that same coward knave Robin Hood. Say, good fellow, wilt thou join my service?"

"Nay, that I will not," quoth the stranger roughly. "I will be mine own, and no man in all merry England shall be my master."

"Then get thee gone, and a plague seize thee!" cried the Sheriff, and his voice trembled with anger. "And by my faith I have a good part of a mind to have thee beaten for thine insolence!" He turned upon his heel and strode away.

Then did Robin and his merry men return to Sherwood Forest. Amidst much laughter, he took the patch from off his eye and stripped away the scarlet rags from off his body and showed himself all clothed in fair Lincoln green.

But Robin Hood took Little John aside and said, "Truly am I vexed, for I heard the Sheriff say today, 'Thou shootest better than that coward knave Robin Hood, that dared not show his face here this day.' I would fain let him know who it was won the golden arrow—and that I am no coward."

Little John said, "Good master, I will send yon fat Sheriff news of all this by a messenger such as he doth not expect."

That day as the Sheriff sat at meat in the great hall of his house, an arrow came through the open window and landed on the dinner table. A fine scroll was tied to it. The Sheriff opened the scroll and glanced at it while the veins upon his forehead swelled and his cheeks grew ruddy with rage, for this is what he saw:

"Now Heaven bless thy Grace this day
    Say all in Sweet Sherwood,
For thou didst give the prize away
    To merry Robin Hood."

The Treasure Hunt

ROBERT LOUIS STEVENSON

Young Jim Hawkins' adventures began when he found a pirate's treasure map. Treasure Island *is Jim's account of how he and his friends hired a ship and crew and set out to find the hidden treasure. Going in search of adventure and gold became dangerous when the crew mutinied and abandoned ship. Their leader was Long John Silver, a cruel, clever pirate who had only one leg and carried a noisy parrot on his shoulder. Jim's friends managed to escape and defend themselves in an old fortress on the island. But Long John Silver forced Jim to follow him and the mutineers in their lusty search for the buried doubloons.*

65

WE HAD THUS PROCEEDED for about half a mile, and were approaching the brow of the plateau, when the man upon the farthest left began to cry aloud, as if in terror. Shout after shout came from him, and the others began to run in his direction.

"He can't 'a' found the treasure," said old Morgan, hurrying past us from the right, "for that's clean a-top."

Indeed, as we found when we also reached the spot, it was something very different. At the foot of a pretty big pine, and involved in a green creeper, which had even partly lifted some of the smaller bones, a human skeleton lay, with a few shreds of clothing, on the ground. I believe a chill struck for a moment to every heart.

"He was a seaman," said George Merry, who, bolder than the rest, had gone up close, and was examining the rags of clothing. "Leastways, this is good sea-cloth."

"Ay, ay," said Silver, "like enough. You wouldn't look to find a bishop here, I reckon. But what sort of a way is that for bones to lie? 'Tain't in nature."

Indeed, on a second glance, it seemed impossible to fancy that the body was in a natural position. But for some disarray, the man lay perfectly straight—his feet pointing in one direction, his hands, raised above his head like a diver's, pointing directly in the opposite.

"I've taken a notion into my old numskull," observed Silver. "Here's the compass. There's the tip-top point o' Skeleton Island, stickin' out like a tooth. Just take a bearing, will you, along the line of them bones."

It was done. The body pointed straight in the direction of the island, and the compass read duly "East South-East by East."

"I thought so," cried the cook. "This here is a pointer. Right up there is our line for the Pole Star and the jolly dollars. But, by thunder! if it don't make me cold inside to think of Flint. This is one of *his* jokes, and no mistake. Him and these six was alone here. He killed 'em, every man, and this one he hauled here, and laid down by compass, shiver my timbers! They're long bones, and the hair's been yellow. Ay, that would be Allardyce."

"There ain't a thing left here," said Merry, feeling round among the bones, "not a copper doit nor a baccy box. It don't look natural to me."

"No, by gum, it don't," agreed Silver, "not natural nor not nice, says you. Great guns, messmates, but if Flint was living, this would be a hot spot for you and me. Six they were, and six are we, and bones is what they are now."

"I saw him dead with these here deadlights," said Morgan. "Billy took me in. There he laid, with penny-pieces on his eyes."

"Dead—ay, sure enough he's dead and gone below," said the fellow with the bandage. "But if ever sperrit walked, it would be Flint's. Dear heart, but he died bad, did Flint!"

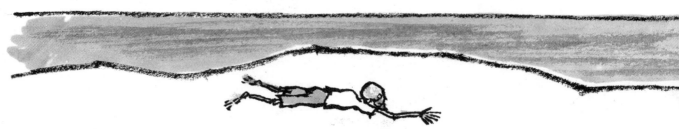

"Ay, that he did," observed another. "Now he raged, and now he hollered for the rum, and now he sang. 'Fifteen Men' were his only song, mates; and I tell you true, I never rightly liked to hear it since. It was main hot, and the windy was open, and I hear that old song comin' out as clear as clear—and the death-haul on the man already."

"Come, come," said Silver, "stow this talk. He's dead, and he don't walk, that I know. Leastways, he won't walk by day, and you may lay to that. Care killed a cat. Fetch ahead for the doubloons."

We started, certainly. But in spite of the hot sun and the staring daylight, the pirates no longer ran separate and shouting through the wood, but kept side by side and spoke with bated breath. The terror of the dead buccaneer had fallen on their spirits.

Humor and Nonsense

What makes you laugh? A funny television show? Jokes? Comic books? Maybe the things that make you laugh don't seem funny at all to your parents or even to your best friend. But some things seem funny to almost everyone.

The next two stories have made all kinds of people laugh. They show two different ways of being funny. Tom Sawyer's story makes you laugh because of the way people (and animals) behave. Alice and Humpty Dumpty are funny because of what they *say*.

If you like these stories, you will probably want to read the entire books about Alice in Wonderland and Tom Sawyer's adventures.

Alice Meets
Humpty Dumpty

LEWIS CARROLL

THE EGG GOT LARGER and larger, and more and more human. When she had come within a few yards of it, she saw that it had eyes and a nose and mouth. And when she had come close to it, she saw clearly that it was Humpty Dumpty himself. "It can't be anybody else!" she said to herself. "I'm as certain of it as if his name were written all over his face."

Humpty Dumpty was sitting with his legs crossed, like a Turk, on the top of a high wall—such a narrow one that Alice quite wondered how he could keep his balance—and, as his eyes were steadily fixed in the opposite direction, and he didn't take the least notice of her, she thought he must be a stuffed figure after all.

"And how exactly like an egg he is!" she said aloud, standing with her hands ready to catch him, for she was every moment expecting him to fall.

"It's *very* provoking," Humpty Dumpty said after a long silence, looking away from Alice as he spoke, "to be called an egg—*very!*"

"I said you *looked* like an egg, Sir," Alice gently explained. "And some eggs are very pretty, you know," she added, hoping to turn her remark into a sort of compliment.

"Some people," said Humpty Dumpty, looking away from her as usual, "have no more sense than a baby!"

Alice didn't know what to say to this. It wasn't at all like conversation, she thought, as he never said

anything to *her*. In fact, his last remark was evidently addressed to a tree—so she stood and softly repeated to herself:

> *Humpty Dumpty sat on a wall:*
> *Humpty Dumpty had a great fall.*
> *All the King's horses and all the King's men*
> *Couldn't put Humpty Dumpty in his place again.*

"That last line is much too long for the poetry," she added, almost out loud, forgetting that Humpty Dumpty would hear her.

"Don't stand chattering to yourself like that," Humpty Dumpty said, looking at her for the first time, "but tell me your name and your business."

"My *name* is Alice, but —"

"It's a stupid name enough!" Humpty Dumpty interrupted impatiently. "What does it mean?"

"Must a name mean something?" Alice asked.

"Of course it must," Humpty Dumpty said with a short laugh. "*My* name means the shape I am—and a good handsome shape it is, too. With a name like yours, you might be any shape, almost."

"Why do you sit out here all alone?" said Alice, not wishing to begin an argument.

"Why, because there's nobody with me!" cried Humpty Dumpty. "Did you think I didn't know the answer to *that*? Ask another."

"Don't you think you'd be safer down on the ground?" Alice went on, not with any idea of making another riddle, but simply in her good-natured anxiety for the queer creature. "That wall is so very narrow!"

"What tremendously easy riddles you ask!" Humpty Dumpty growled out. "Of course I don't think so! Why, if ever I *did* fall off—which there's no chance of—but *if* I did—" Here he pursed up his lips and looked so solemn and grand that Alice could hardly help laughing. "*If* I did fall," he went on, "the King has promised me— ah, you may turn pale, if you like! The King has promised me, with his very own mouth, to—"

"To send all his horses and all his men," Alice interrupted, rather unwisely.

"Now I declare that's too bad!" Humpty Dumpty cried, breaking into a sudden passion. "You've been listening at doors, and behind trees, and down chimneys, or you couldn't have known it!"

"I haven't, indeed!" Alice said very gently. "It's in a book."

"Ah, well! They may write such things in a *book*," Humpty Dumpty said in a calmer tone. "That's what you call a History of England, that is. Now, take a good look at me! I'm one that has spoken to a King, *I* am.

Mayhap you'll never see such another, and to show you I'm not proud, you may shake hands with me!" And he grinned almost from ear to ear, as he leant forwards (and as nearly as possible fell off the wall in doing so) and offered Alice his hand.

She watched him a little anxiously as she took it. "If he smiled much more, the ends of his mouth might meet behind," she thought, "and then I don't know what would happen to his head! I'm afraid it would come off!"

"Yes, all his horses and all his men," Humpty Dumpty went on. "They'd pick me up again in a minute, they would! However, this conversation is going on a little too fast. Let's go back to the last remark but one."

"I'm afraid I can't quite remember it," Alice said very politely.

"In that case we start fresh," said Humpty Dumpty, "and it's my turn to choose a subject." ("He talks about it just as if it was a game!" thought Alice.) "So here's a question for you. How old did you say you were?"

Alice made a short calculation, and said "Seven years and six months."

"Wrong!" Humpty Dumpty exclaimed triumphantly. "You never said a word like it!"

"I thought you meant 'How old are you?'" Alice explained.

"If I'd meant that, I'd have said it," said Humpty Dumpty.

Alice didn't want to begin another argument, so she said nothing.

"Seven years and six months!" Humpty Dumpty repeated thoughtfully. "An uncomfortable sort of age. Now if you'd asked *my* advice, I'd have said 'Leave off at seven'—but it's too late now."

"I never ask advice about growing," Alice said indignantly.

"Too proud?" the other enquired.

Alice felt even more indignant at this suggestion. "I mean," she said, "that one can't help growing older."

"*One* can't, perhaps," said Humpty Dumpty, "but *two* can. With proper assistance, you might have left off at seven."

"What a beautiful belt you've got on!" Alice suddenly remarked. (They had had quite enough of the subject of age, she thought, and if they really were to take turns in choosing subjects, it was her turn now.) "At least," she corrected herself on second thoughts, "a beautiful cravat, I should have said—no, a belt, I mean—I beg your pardon!" she added in dismay, for Humpty Dumpty looked thoroughly offended, and she began to wish she hadn't chosen that subject. "If only I knew," she thought to herself, "which was neck and which was waist!"

Evidently Humpty Dumpty was very angry, though he said nothing for a minute or two. When he *did* speak again, it was in a deep growl.

"It is a most provoking thing," he said at last, "when a person doesn't know a cravat from a belt!"

"I know it's very ignorant of me," Alice said, in so humble a tone that Humpty Dumpty relented.

"It's a cravat, child, and a beautiful one, as you say. It's a present from the White King and Queen!"

"Is it really?" said Alice, quite pleased to find that she *had* chosen a good subject, after all.

"They gave it me," Humpty Dumpty continued thoughtfully, as he crossed one knee over the other and clasped his hands round it, "they gave it me—for an un-birthday present."

"I beg your pardon?" Alice said with a puzzled air.

"I'm not offended," said Humpty Dumpty.

"I mean, what *is* an un-birthday present?"

"A present given when it isn't your birthday, of course," Humpty Dumpty answered.

Alice considered a little. "I like birthday presents best," she said at last.

"You don't know what your're talking about!" cried Humpty Dumpty. "How many days are there in a year?"

"Three hundred and sixty-five," said Alice.

"And how many birthdays have you?"

"One."

"And if you take one from three hundred and sixty-five, what remains?"

"Three hundred and sixty-four, of course."

Humpty Dumpty looked doubtful. "I'd rather see that done on paper," he said.

Alice couldn't help smiling as she took out her memorandum-book, and worked the sum for him:

$$365$$

$$\underline{1}$$

$$364$$

Humpty Dumpty took the book, and looked at it carefully. "That seems to be done right," he began.

"You're holding it upside down!" Alice interrupted.

"To be sure I was!" Humpty Dumpty said gaily, as she turned it round for him. "I thought it looked a little queer. As I was saying, that *seems* to be done right—though I haven't time to look it over thoroughly just now—and that shows that there are three hundred and sixty-four days when you might get un-birthday presents. And only *one* for birthday presents, you know!"

The Cat
and the Pain-Killer

MARK TWAIN

The Adventures of Tom Sawyer *tells the story of a boy who grew up in a small town on the Mississippi River about 100 years ago. Tom and his friends really did have adventures — they got lost in a cave, they were witnesses in a murder trial, and one time they even disappeared on an island in the river. During all this, Tom lived with his Aunt Polly who, at times, found Tom's shenanigans more than she could handle.*

TOM'S MIND HAD DRIFTED away from its secret troubles. It had found a new and weighty matter to interest itself about. Becky Thatcher had stopped coming to school. Tom had struggled with his pride a few days, and tried to "whistle her down the wind," but failed. He began to find himself hanging around her father's house, nights, and feeling very miserable. She was ill. What if she should die? There was distraction in the thought. He no longer took an interest in war, nor even in piracy. He put his hoop away and his bat; there was no joy in them any more. His aunt was concerned.

She began to try all manner of remedies on him. She was one of those people who are infatuated with patent medicines and all new-fangled methods of producing

health or mending it. She was an inveterate experimenter in these things. When something fresh in this line came out she was in a fever, right away, to try it—not on herself, for she was never ailing, but on anybody else that came handy. She was a subscriber for all the "Health" periodicals. The solemn ignorance they were inflated with was breath to her nostrils. She never observed that her health journals of the current month customarily upset everything they had recommended the month before. She was as simple-hearted and honest as the day is long and so she was an easy victim.

The water treatment was new now, and Tom's low condition was a windfall to her. She had him out at daylight every morning, stood him up in the woodshed and drowned him with a deluge of cold water. Then she scrubbed him down with a towel like a file, and so brought him to. Then she rolled him up in a wet sheet and put him away under blankets till she sweated his soul clean and "the yellow stains of it came through his pores"—as Tom said.

Yet notwithstanding all this, the boy grew more and more melancholy and pale and dejected. She added hot baths, sitz baths, shower baths, and plunges. The boy remained as dismal as a hearse. She began to assist the water with a slim oatmeal diet and blister-plasters. She calculated his capacity as she would a jug's, and filled him up every day with quack cure-alls.

Tom had become indifferent to persecution by this time. This phase filled the old lady's heart with consternation. This indifference must be broken up at any cost. Now she heard of Pain-killer for the first time. She ordered a lot at once. She tasted it and was filled with gratitude. It was simply fire in a liquid form. She dropped the water treatment and everything else, and pinned her faith to Pain-killer. She gave Tom a teaspoonful and watched with the deepest anxiety for the result. Her troubles were instantly at rest, her soul at peace again, for the "indifference" was broken up. The boy could not have shown a wilder, heartier interest if she had built a fire under him.

Tom felt that it was time to wake up. This sort of life might be romantic enough, in his blighted condition, but it was getting to have too little sentiment and too much distracting variety about it. So he thought over various plans for relief, and finally hit upon that of professing to be fond of Pain-killer. He asked for it so often that he became a nuisance, and his aunt ended by telling him to help himself and quit bothering her. If it had been Sid, she would have had no misgivings to alloy her delight; but since it was Tom, she watched the bottle clandestinely. She found that the medicine did really diminish, but it did not occur to her that the boy was mending the health of a crack in the sitting-room floor with it.

One day Tom was in the act of dosing the crack when his aunt's yellow cat came along, purring, eyeing the teaspoon avariciously, and begging for a taste. Tom said: "Don't ask for it unless you want it, Peter."

But Peter signified that he did want it.

"You better make sure."

Peter was sure.

"Now you've asked for it, and I'll give it to you, because there ain't anything mean about *me*. But if you find you don't like it, you mustn't blame anybody but your own self."

Peter was agreeable. So Tom pried his mouth open and poured down the Pain-killer. Peter sprang a couple of yards in the air, and then delivered a war-whoop and set off round and round the room, banging against furniture, upsetting flower pots, and making general havoc. Next he rose on his hind feet and pranced around, in a

frenzy of enjoyment, with his head over his shoulder and his voice proclaiming his unappeasable happiness. Then he went tearing around the house again, spreading chaos and destruction in his path. Aunt Polly entered in time to see him throw a few double somersaults, deliver a final mighty hurrah, and sail through the open window, carrying the rest of the flower pots with him. The old lady stood petrified with astonishment, peering over her glasses. Tom lay on the floor expiring with laughter.

"Tom, what on earth ails that cat?"

"*I* don't know, aunt," gasped the boy.

"Why, I never see anything like it. What *did* make him act so?"

"'Deed I don't know, Aunt Polly. Cats always act so when they're having a good time."

"They do, do they?" There was something in the tone that made Tom apprehensive.

"Yes'm. That is, I believe they do."

"You *do?*"

"Yes'm!"

The old lady was bending down, Tom watching, with interest emphasized by anxiety. Too late he divined her drift. The handle of the telltale teaspoon was visible under the bed valance. Aunt Polly took it, held it up. Tom winced, and dropped his eyes. Aunt Polly raised him by the usual handle—his ear—and cracked his head soundly with her thimble.

"Now, sir, what did you want to treat that poor dumb beast so for?"

"I done it out of pity for him—because he hadn't any aunt."

"Hadn't any aunt!—you numskull. What has that got to do with it?"

"Heaps. Because if he'd 'a' had one she'd 'a' burnt him out herself! She'd 'a' roasted his bowels out of him 'thout any more feeling than if he was a human!"

Aunt Polly felt a sudden pang of remorse. This was putting the thing in a new light. What was cruelty to a cat *might* be cruelty to a boy, too. She began to soften; she felt sorry. Her eyes watered a little, and she put her hand on Tom's head and said gently:

"I was meaning for the best, Tom. And, Tom, it *did* do you good."

Tom looked up in her face with just a perceptible twinkle peeping through his gravity.

"I know you was meaning for the best, auntie, and so was I with Peter. It done *him* good, too. I never see him get around so since—"

"Oh, go 'long with you, Tom, before you aggravate me again. And you try and see if you can't be a good boy, for once, and you needn't take any more medicine.

Poems

Songs are poetry. So are nursery rhymes
and Mother Goose rhymes. In fact, poetry
is almost anything that has a swing, or
rhythm to it.

Two of these poems tell how the poets who
wrote them felt about being outdoors. One
is a bedtime story written as a poem. And
one tells the story of a brave old lady
during the Civil War.

In other books you can find many poems
that tell stories, and many others that tell
about times when a poet felt happy or
sad, joyful or lonely.

Read poetry out loud so that you can hear
the "swing" and the sounds of the words.
Or ask someone else to read poems to you
so you can just listen.

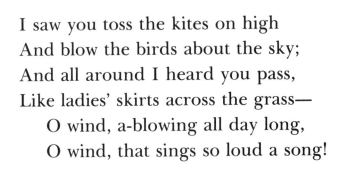

I saw you toss the kites on high
And blow the birds about the sky;
And all around I heard you pass,
Like ladies' skirts across the grass—
 O wind, a-blowing all day long,
 O wind, that sings so loud a song!

The Wind

I saw the different things you did,
But always you yourself you hid.
I felt you push, I heard you call,
I could not see yourself at all—
 O wind, a-blowing all day long,
 O wind, that sings so loud a song!

O you that are so strong and cold,
O blower, are you young or old?
Are you a beast of field and tree,
Or just a stronger child than me?
 O wind, a-blowing all day long,
 O wind, that sings so loud a song!

ROBERT LOUIS STEVENSON

Sound the flute!
Now it's mute.
Birds delight
Day and Night;
Nightingale
In the dale,
Lark in Sky,
Merrily,
Merrily, merrily, to welcome in the Year.

Little Boy,
Full of joy;
Little Girl,
Sweet and small;
Cock does crow,
So do you;
Merry voice,
Infant noise,
Merrily, merrily, to welcome in the Year.

Spring

Little Lamb
Here I am;
Come and lick
My white neck;
Let me pull
Your soft Wool;
Let me kiss
Your soft face;
Merrily, merrily, we welcome in the Year.

WILLIAM BLAKE

Wynken, Blynken, and Nod one night
  Sailed off in a wooden shoe—
Sailed on a river of crystal light,
  Into a sea of dew.
"Where are you going, and what do you wish?"
  The old moon asked the three.
"We have come to fish for the herring fish
  That live in this beautiful sea;
  Nets of silver and gold have we!"
      Said Wynken,
      Blynken,
      And Nod.

Wynken,
Blynken, and
Nod

The old moon laughed and sang a song,
  As they rocked in the wooden shoe,
And the wind that sped them all night long
  Ruffled the waves of dew.
The little stars were the herring fish
  That lived in that beautiful sea—
"Now cast your nets wherever you wish—
  Never afeard are we";
  So cried the stars to the fishermen three:
      Wynken,
      Blynken,
      And Nod.

All night long their nets they threw
   To the stars in the twinkling foam—
Then down from the skies came the wooden shoe,
   Bringing the fishermen home;
'Twas all so pretty a sail it seemed
   As if it could not be,
And some folks thought 'twas a dream they'd dreamed
   Of sailing that beautiful sea—
   But I shall name you the fishermen three:
         Wynken,
         Blynken,
         And Nod.

Wynken and Blynken are two little eyes,
   And Nod is a little head,
And the wooden shoe that sailed the skies
   Is a wee one's trundle-bed.
So shut your eyes while mother sings
   Of wonderful sights that be,
And you shall see the beautiful things
   As you rock in the misty sea,
   Where the old shoe rocked the fishermen three:
         Wynken,
         Blynken,
         And Nod.

EUGENE FIELD

Barbara Frietchie

Up from the meadows rich with corn,
Clear in the cool September morn,

The clustered spires of Frederick stand
Green-walled by the hills of Maryland.

Round about them orchards sweep,
Apple and peach tree fruited deep,

Fair as the garden of the Lord
To the eyes of the famished rebel horde,

On that pleasant morn of the early fall
When Lee marched over the mountain wall;

Over the mountains winding down,
Horse and foot, into Frederick town.

Up rose old Barbara Frietchie then,
Bowed with her fourscore years and ten;

Bravest of all in Frederick town,
She took up the flag the men hauled down;

In her attic window the staff she set,
To show that one heart was loyal yet.

Up the street came the rebel tread,
Stonewall Jackson riding ahead.

Under his slouched hat left and right
He glanced; the old flag met his sight.

"Halt!"—the dust-brown ranks stood fast,
"Fire!"—out blazed the rifle-blast.

It shivered the window, pane and sash;
It rent the banner with seam and gash.

Quick as it fell, from the broken staff
Dame Barbara snatched the silken scarf.

She leaned far out on the window-sill,
And shook it forth with a royal will.

"Shoot, if you must, this old gray head,
But spare your country's flag," she said.

A shade of sadness, a blush of shame,
Over the face of the leader came;

The nobler nature within him stirred
To life at that woman's deed and word;

"Who touches a hair of yon gray head
Dies like a dog! March on!" he said.

All day long through Frederick street
Sounded the tread of marching feet:

All day long that free flag tossed
Over the heads of the rebel host.

Barbara Frietchie's work is o'er,
And the Rebel rides on his raids no more.

Over Barbara Frietchie's grave,
Flag of Freedom and Union, wave!

And ever the stars above look down
On thy stars below in Frederick town!

JOHN GREENLEAF WHITTIER